Adharlal Sen

Shrines of Sitakund

Adharlal Sen

Shrines of Sitakund

ISBN/EAN: 9783337385354

Printed in Europe, USA, Canada, Australia, Japan

Cover: Foto ©Andreas Hilbeck / pixelio.de

More available books at **www.hansebooks.com**

THE

SHRINES OF SITAKUND

IN THE DISTRICT OF

CHITTAGONG IN BENGAL

BY

ADHARLAL SEN, B. A.

DEPUTY COLLECTOR OF CALCUTTA, FORMERLY OF CHITTAGONG.
LATE SCHOLAR, PRESIDENCY COLLEGE; MEMBER OF THE
ASIATIC SOCIETY OF BENGAL; AUTHOR OF "LALITA
SUNDARI," "MENAKA," "NALINI," "KUSUM KANAN,"
AND "LYTTONIANA;" FELLOW OF THE
UNIVERSITY OF CALCUTTA.

CALCUTTA

THACKER, SPINK & CO.

Publishers to the University.

1884.

PREFACE.

I visited Sitakund in 1880, during the *Siva-Chaturdasi* festival. From the notes then recorded by me, I wrote a paper on the Shrines of the place, which was read before the Asiatic Society of Bengal on the 2nd March, 1881. This paper, with some additions and alterations, is now presented before the public.

It was owing to the kindness of the late Pandit Bhairava Chandra Nyayaratna of Chittagong, that I was able to obtain copies of some of the sacred writings to which reference is made in the following pages. To my old and revered tutor, Pandit Haris Chandra Kaviratna, of the Presidency College, my thanks are also due for his kindly going through the proofsheets, and helping me with his suggestions.

A. S.

Calcutta, June 15th, 1884.

SHRINES OF SITAKUND.

Sitákund is an outpost in the Police circle of Kumiria attached to the Sudder Subdivision of the district of Chittagong in Bengal. It is bounded on the east by the Sitakund range, on the west by the Bay of Bengal, on the north and south by the Kumiria and Merkaserai thanas respectively, the population by the last Census being 86,581 souls.

The city of the same name (lat. 22° 37' 55"; long. 91° 48' 40"), which is at a distance of 24 miles to the north of the Sudder Station, is not mentioned by name in the Ayeen Akbery; but it appears to have been a place of considerable importance at the time when Chittagong first came into the possession of the English. Mr. Harry Verelst, the first Chief of Chittagong, who afterwards succeeded Mr. Vansittart in the Governorship of Bengal, reported his arrival from this place on the 3rd January, 1761.* Lord

* Mr. Cotton's Memorandum on the Revenue History of Chittagong, page 5.

1

Teignmouth visited it in 1778,[*] and Sir William
Jones in 1786.[†] It was also inspected and described
by Captain Pogson in 1831,[‡] and Sir Joseph Hooker
in 1854.[§] Sitakund still continues to hold its position as a place of note in the district. It has a
moonsifee of its own, which, though still going by
its name, has, however, been recently removed to an
adjacent place. The trade of Sitakund is not incon-
siderable, lying as it does on the Grand Trunk Road
between Dacca and Chittagong, which is always fit
for wheeled traffic, and being accessible within a
short distance by boats throughout the year. There
is not certainly a more beautiful place on earth.
Nature has adorned it with all that is sublime and
beautiful in creation. It is a meet residence for
gods. The grand mountains, the beautiful water-
falls, the volcanic springs, the clear streams, the
thick forests, and their conflagrations at night, the
numberless odorous flowers, the fragrant breeze and
the sweet song of birds,—these no one can forget,
who has once been there.

[*] Lord Teignmouth's Memoirs of Sir William Jones, Vol. II, p. 55.

[†] Ibid. Letter from Sir William Jones to Mr. Justice Hyde.

[‡] Pogson's Narrative during a Tour to Chateegaon, p. 204. The
date of Pogson's visit to Sitakund, as given by the late Dr. Oldham,
quoting Corbyn, in his paper on the Thermal Springs of India edited
by his son, is 1778. (*Vide* p. 59, Part II, Vol. XIX. Memoirs of
the Geological Survey of India.) But this is not correct, as will be
seen from Captain Pogson's own Narrative. It was Lord Teignmouth who visited the place in 1778.

[§] Hooker's Himalayan Journals, Vol. II, p. 352.

It is, however, from a religious point of view, that the place is held in the greatest esteem. In Eastern Bengal, which is condemned by the orthodox as the Mleccha country, not visited by the Pándavas (पाण्डवविलेपदेश), there is no place so renowned as Sitakund. It is one of the 51 sacred Píthas (पीठ),* on which fell scattered the limbs of Satí, the consort of Siva, whose dead body was cut to pieces by the discus of Vishnu. "On Chandrasekhara in Chittagong in Eastern Bengal," says the Ádipuréna,† "there is a place of great sanctity, which

* चाहवे दृवनाङ्गनो मिरबचन्द्रमे खरः ।
आत्मरूपा अवक्षमी अवानी तम दैवता ॥

इति मन्त्रचूडामणो रिवपार्वतीयेवाहे
रखपूजादिदोषमौ पौठविर्येषः ।

Vide Sir Raja Radhakanta Deva's Sabdakalpadruma, Vol. III, p. 2150, and Vol. VII, p. 703 (supplement) 1st Edition.

चतुर्धामे जानिहइ धर्म अनुभव ।
उवानी नेवता चन्द्रलेखर त्रिभव ॥

भारतचन्द्र राजेन्द्र अन्नदामङ्गल ।
अन्नवारेर्र् १म निशा पाला ।

Date of composition of *Annaddmangala*, S. 1674=1753 A. D.

वेद मदर धवि रजन युक्त विज्ञपिला ।
लेइ शके एइ गीत धारव रचिला ॥

† इवाभिक्षवितां वोष नक्षवाद् पाव्वि मेखले ।
व्यतिनुष्ठं नवसुष्ठं चाहवे चन्द्रमेखरे ॥

Ádipuréna, Vide. p. 105 Chandrasekhara Máhátmya by Uma Charan Mookerjee.

is the favourite and secret resort of the gods." "We
have heard before," the Rishis said in the *Devípurána*,*
"of Sitakund situate on the mount of Chandrasekhara,
a spring known throughout India, which is the purifier of the three worlds". "Ayodhya, Muttra, Maya
(Hurdwar), Benares, Kánchi (Conjeveram), Avanti
(Ojjein), and Dwáraká—these seven places are the dis-
pensers of salvation. In Benares, Maináka, Ekámra-
vana (Bhubanesvara), Kailás and Sumeru, Siva
constantly dwells. During the Kali Yuga," says
Vishnu to his consort, in the *Váráhi Tantra*,† "Chittagong is the habitation of the gods." So again Siva
said in the *Linga Purana*,‡ "I shall dwell with thee, O

* रोगाकुषं गुलं पूर्ं वेद्वोक्त्वजनपावनं ।
चन्द्रमेश्वरमखवं भारताख्याससम्बिलम् ॥
इति नोदेनोपुरावे पेषमाषाद्ये चष्चिंत्राण्डे षिवरज्ज-
कचने योनोचन्द्रमेश्वरमाप्तिरद्धाद्मोऽध्याकः ।

† अयोध्या मथुरा माया काशी काञ्ची अवन्तिका ।
पुरी द्वारावती चैव सप्तेमा मुक्तिदायिका ॥
वारावती च मैनाक एकाम्रवनमेव च ।
कैलासरजतादिच सर्वोत्रित्त्यन्ववः ॥
एवेषु अकुरो निल्यं सर्वेदेषोषनम्विलः ।
कलौ आगच्छ सर्वेषां रेवालां वहसे धुमे ॥
इति योवारावौनमें योगारायचनारायपचौर्षगाते
ज्ञीषा पठका ।

‡ श्रीकालाय पिलाजीव वसते चन्द्रमेश्वरे ।
यथा तव वसिष्यामि ततं तत्व वरागमे ॥

                    Linga Purana, *Vide.* p. 105, Chandrasekhara Máhát-
mya by Uma Charan Mookerjea.

fair-faced one, on Chandrasekhara in Bengal for the good of men." The sanctity of the shrines of Sita-kund is a favourite theme with the writers of the Puranas and Tantras, and passages bearing on the subject need not be multiplied. The shrines attract pilgrims from all parts of Bengal, Behar, and Orissa, as also from the North-Western Provinces. The Siva-Chaturdasí festival, according to Dr. Hunter,[*] is at-tended by ten to twenty thousand pilgrims. The mi-nor gatherings, at the eclipses of the sun and moon, and at like occasions, number from two to four thou-sand devotees.

The leading works which treat of these shrines are (1) *Devípuránа*, (2) *Váráhí Tantra*, (3) *Ǫhinna-mastá Tantra*. Passing mention of them may also be found in the following works: *Ádipurana, Linga Purana, A'di Brahma Purana, Churámani Tantra, Yogini Tantra, Váyu Purana, Bhavishya Purana, Tantrasára*, and *Kálimáhátmya*. A passage "अमृताम्-लिलिला लिल्ल लिल्लिल लिल्लाल लिल्लिला"is generally referred to the *Amara-kosha*. In Colebrooke's excellent edition of the Dic-tionary, I searched for the passage in vain, but have succeeded in tracing it to the *Mahálingesvara Tantra* in the prayer of a hundred names addressed to Siva. The exact age, in which the aforesaid Tantras and Puranas were written, cannot be ascer-tained. According to Dr. Monier Williams, " if the oldest known Purana is not older than the sixth or

[*] *Vide* Hunter's Statistical Account of Chittagong, p. 222.

seventh century, an earlier date can scarcely be attributed to the oldest known Tantra."[*] There is no mention of Chittagong, or of the shrines of Sitakund, either in the *Rámáyana*, or in the *Mahábhárata*. According to Dr. Hunter,[†] there is mention in the latter epic of Triloobana, a powerful king of Tipperah, who is supposed to have been contemporary with Yudhishthira; but I have failed to trace it, though I came across two passages which speak of the conquest of that kingdom by Sahadeva and Karna.[‡] We also know that the early kings of Tipperah were staunch Sivaites, and that a portion of the expenses of the Sitakund shrines is still defrayed by the Tipperah Raj.[§] Dr. Hunter[||] has also informed. us, that "in 1512 the Tipperah General conquered Chittagong." But when these shrines, now so cele-

---

[*] Dr. Monier Williams's Indian Wisdom, page 504.

[†] Hunter's Statistical Account of Hill Tipperah, page 484.

[‡] वेपुरं जनमे ह्ना राजामनमितौजसम् ।
    विजयाय नयामांडरएता पौरवेश्वरम् ॥ ८८॥
        इति व्याप्यर्वेपि दिग्विजयपर्वेपि उत्तरेपदिग्विजये
                    रत्रविंशताधोऽध्यायः ।

    मौपर्व पतनद्वैव तिपुरां कोहयतां गवा ।
    एतान् एवान् विनिर्जिल्य वरभाहाय एवैग्र ॥ ८ ॥
    दपिवा दिग्मोआक्षाय कर्वी जिला भवारएवान् ।
    वर्जिग्वं दानिपवात्येन योग्यवाहाव इतनः ॥ १० ॥
        इत्यारण्यके पर्वेपि योग्यावाचापर्वेपि सर्वदिग्विजये
                    विपद्याग्रद्विद्विशतनमोऽध्यायः ।

[§] Baboo Kailas Chandra Sinha's Chronicles of Tipperah, p. 5.

[||] Hunter's Statistical Account of Hill Tipperah, p. 485.

brated, were first established, has not yet been determined. It is remarkable that they were not visited by Hwen Thsang, the Chinese traveller, nor even by the great Chaitanya who is known to have made a pilgrimage to all the known shrines of his time. There can, however, be no doubt as to their recent establishment. Most of the shrines are supposed to have become endued with merit, only in the Kali Yuga. Among the springs mentioned by Captain Pogson in 1831, is Chandur or Chandra Kund, "said to have appeared within the last four months."[*] In a list of objects of antiquarian interest issued by the Government of Bengal, it is said that the temple of Sambhunath was built about 450 years ago, and that of Bárabakunda about 400 years ago, but on what evidence I cannot say.[†]

Sitakund (Spring of Sita) derives its name from a spring consecrated to Sita, the deified heroine of the Rámáyana. The spring, however, is no longer in existence. A tradition prevails, that there was at one time a dispute between the followers of Vishnu and Siva about the possession of the spring, and that the dispute was referred for arbitration to one Kali Charan Roy, a zemindar and dewan in the

[*] Captain Pogson's Narrative during a Tour to Chatesgaon, p. 204.

[†] A List of the Objects of Antiquarian Interest in the Lower Provinces of Bengal compiled at the Bengal Secretariat under the orders of the Government of India, 1879.

local Collectorate,* who, it is said, caused the spring
to be filled up to terminate the difference. According to another account, the destruction of the spring
was effected by the then Mohunta of Sitakund.
The present Mohunta informed me that he had
made several attempts to restore the sacred place,
but that, though he had dug deep all around the
site indicated by the sacred books, he could find
no trace of the spring. His belief was, that there
had been at the place no such spring as is described
in the sacred books, and he told me as a reason for
this belief, that the place in question was found
devoid of all trace of bitumen which was found by
him in the adjacent hot springs.†

* Kali Charan Roy was dewan of the Chittagong Collectorate
from 1785 to 1790. He was one of the farmers with whom Mr. God-
win concluded the Settlement in 1774 On the 5th January, 1786, Mr.
Crofts, who at that time was Collector of Chittagong, sold his right,
title, and interest in the island of Moiscal, for Rs. 40,000 to Kali
Charan Roy. The latter was succeeded in the property by his widow
Probhabaty, who did not die till 1826. She had no children of her
own, but adopted one Chundy Churn, who died in 1820, leaving a
son, Shorut Chunder. Shorut being a minor, the estate came, on
Probhabaty's death, under the Court of Wards. Shorut Chunder
died recently, and the present zemindar is his son, Koilash Chunder. Vide Mr. Cotton's Memorandum on the Revenue History of
Chittagong, pages 155-6, and page 229.

† When this paper was read before the Asiatic Society of Bengal,
Mr. V. Ball remarked that though it may be true that there never
was a hot spring in the locality mentioned, the absence of any trace
of bitumen was no proof of its non-existence. Vide Proceedings of
the Asiatic Society of Bengal for March, 1881, page 51.

Captain Pogson described Sitakund* as "of pure limpid water," though Bárabakunda is the only spring he actually visited. He, however, subsequently obtained information of the other springs, and sent a careful person to bring a description and some bottles of water from each. The following account quoted by Captain Pogson from a *Gazetteer* is noteworthy :† "About twenty miles to the north of Islamabad is a remarkable hot well (named Seetacoond), the surface of which may be inflamed by the application of fire. Like all other remarkable phenomena of nature, it is esteemed sacred by the Hindoos, as is likewise another hot spring near to Monghir." As will presently be seen, the spring of Sitakund is described in the *Devipurana* as hot-watered and igneous, which agrees with the above extract from the *Gazetteer*. But as Sitakund is also the name of the outpost containing all the groups of springs and shrines at the locality, I think it is unsafe to conclude, that the specific spring Sitakund existed at the time when the passages above referred to were written.‡ If the

* Captain Pogson's Narrative during a Tour to Chateogaon, p 204.
† Ibid, page 99.
‡ The popular belief is, that the spring of Sitakund is still in existence. In his clever novel, called Chandranath after the god on the Chandrasekhara hill, the second edition of which appeared last year, Baboo Khottra Pal Chakravarti makes the hero visit Sitakund (p. 208) in 1266 B. S, that is, about 25 years ago All old persons, however, who have visited the place, agree in saying that the spring has not been in existence for a much longer time. Baraba-

spring existed in 1881, at the time when Captain
Pogson wrote his Narrative, it must have been destroyed in recent times.   But the destruction of a
spring, held in such an esteem by the Hindoos, would
not have failed to attract the notice of the authori-
ties.   I am not aware of any official report regarding the destruction of the spring.

The following account is given in the *Devipurana**
of the shrine, and of its destruction :

40-41.—The Rishis said : We have heard before of
Sitakund, situate on the mount of Chandrasekhara, a
spring known throughout India, which is the purifier
of the three worlds.   If thou hast any kindness for
us, O sun of knowledge, do thou tell us of it, and
thereby dispel our ignorance; for about this people
ask of us.

42-8.—The Suta replied : For the performance of

kunda, and not Sitakund, is about 20 miles to the north of Chittagong.

* जनपद जपु । ।

सीताकुर्षं मुनं पूर्षं विशेाकजनपावनम् ।
वन्द्रशेखरलेख्यर्षं भारताख्यासमन्वितम् ॥ ४० ॥
यदि वैशि क्षपा माय मदुह ज्ञानभाष्कर ।
वकाख्यमज्ञानम् पर लीखे इच्छा वदौदमी ॥ ४१ ॥

         सूत उवाच ।

सीतासानविधानार्षं सीतासानाद् पावनात् वै ।
मयामुष्य मयारख्यं मद् ब्रह्मनु विनिर्मितम् ॥ ४२ ॥
याजुवाधिविधिमियनु निजमुण्णेादर्षं प्रिजाः ।
वानपवाचितं मुखैः सर्वोपवनविज्ञम् ॥ ४३ ॥

Sita's ablution, O twice-born ones, and for the purifi-
cation of men, was made that spring, the most secret
and beautiful, volcanic, deep, hot-watered, surrounded
by trees as by an umbrella, forming one continuous
grove.

44.—In that lake bathed Sítá, born of the Earth,
with her husband and brother-in-law, and devoutly
offered oblations to her favourite deity.

45.—There also bathed the lions among the twice-
born, as also the chiefs of sages and Munis, who have
attained perfection, dwelling to the north of it.

46.—What account shall I give of this spring, the
most sanctifying of all? I shall only recount its
merits : listen to me, O most excellent of the twice-
born.

47.—When Ráma, debarred from accession to his
father's throne, had gone to the hermitage of S'arabhanga, he went, in accordance with his direction, to
a city lying towards the north-east.

यच सीता इधिवौला चामिला देवरेव च ।
चामा तच ष्रदे देवजिलं चकायें चकमः ॥ ४४ ॥
चालं चत्रुः द्विजवात्रा मुनिहन्दारेखाखया ।
चिवा मदर्षयः उत्ति तखोतारनिवाचिनः ॥ ४५ ॥
कि मक्तव्यं कृष्ण्डस्य मरापुखचिभावकम् ।
चख्याचि तच्च माचाख्या ष्रयुधे द्विजचुच्चमा ॥ ४६ ॥
राख्यार्चो चदा राजः मरभाचमं चचौ ।
तदुपदेचं चक्ता तु पूर्वौत्तरतुरौनमात् ॥ ४० ॥

48-9.—In that city he saw a revered sage, versed in the knowledge of *Tirthas*, a veritable ocean of knowledge, long-armed, clad in yellow garments, and with matted hair. As soon as he saw him, he reverently saluted him with a meek heart, and enquired of him, "Why dost thou, O Lord, live here alone, besmeared with ashes?"

50-51.—That sage, whose whole body was besmeared with ashes, then opening his eyes, saw Rama, the holy, the eternal, the best of men, accompanied by Sita and Lakshmana, and thus addressed him:

52.—"I have heard that thou hast taken thy birth in the line of kings, only for our liberation from the dire bonds of the world.

53-4.—"How great is thy fortune, who art followed

पश्येत् एवं अद्वापार्श्व अद्वासच्चद्वधारिवम् ।
शीतवक्षपरीधानं नौ भंभं ज्ञानवागरम् ॥ ४८ ॥
इष्टा नमा च पश्यन् भक्ता विनयमागतः ।
अवमन् जितं देवमर्तितं विभ्रमिवरम् ॥ ४९ ॥
तमच्छुरक्षीकथिता इष्टा दार्षं उनानवम् ।
ज्ञानकौच्छक्षदाश्रान्तु पविवं पुरुषोत्तमम् ॥ ५० ॥
चरोचन एवुवर्त उ मुनिर्विभ्रमिवरः ।
ष्रुतं राजन्यवंभे तु अन्नमात्रप्रतिष्ठितम् ॥ ५१ ॥
वद्वान् पविवकरवे नौरद्वंसारवस्मनात् ।
आपन्नानं मुक्ति कुर्वन् नौके अस्य प्रकाशितम् ॥ ५२ ॥
एवं नीता प्रविनौजा कर्क्षिवित्विन्वसंखिता ।
इरारात्था मुक्तकेशी चापवर्नप्रदायिनी ॥ ५३ ॥
यथानुनामिनी एषो नख्य भाग्यं प्रतिष्ठितम् ।
वल्लुमक्षीगरे नौरे भारताज्ञावनम्विते ॥ ५४ ॥

by this Sita, born of the Earth, with her hair un-
bound, the dispenser of salvation, worshipped even
by Siva.

55.—"On the north side of the Indian Sea, there is
a spring bearing her name, well known throughout
India, which is the purifier of the three worlds.
Know her not merely as thy wife. Verily she is
Yoganidrá herself.

56.—"Deeds unaccomplishable by thee can easily
be achieved by her; she is destined by the Fates to
humiliate thy pride (to eclipse thy glory).

57-60.—"It is through my good fortune alone, O
Rama, that thou hast come here with her. On the
mount of Chandrasekhara, southwest of this country,
was built by Siva, a spring of her name. Behold that
spring, Sitakund, glowing with fire, situate on the
west of S'ambhunath, south of the Vayu hills, north of

वक्ता माजा कृतमकि चिन्नोकजनपायनम् ।
न मव रहिबी राम यौमनिद्रेयमिख्ये ॥ ५५ ॥
तवायक्यं कर्म वड्ढा बनदावचौकाकमम् ।
तयाभिमाने महे य विधिनैषा निवोजिता ॥ ५६ ॥
मम भाव्यवस्राह्मम् बलवा वमुपस्थितः ।
प्रायौदविवचलोमंधे मौचन्द्रमेकरे गिरौ ॥ ५७ ॥
नप अनेष नम्नाखा कृतबलेबं निवोजितम् ।
लयमुपविले चिम्राक्ततायुविरिदस्थिये ॥ ५८ ॥
भाभिमत्रीतरे षैव वक्नुपविमत् स्थितः ।
बोतिलैयाबः मतौर्या बाब्वायिवलन्बितम् ॥ ५९ ॥
पम्रेव य मम्राकुर्ब बौनागाखा निवोजितम् ।
बौला मौमकपुत्ना या षैवले इवचारिवौ ॥ ६० ॥

Nábhigangá, west of the Phalgu, below Jyotirmaya.
That Sita is thy cheering consort."

61-3.—Thus speaking, the excellent sage fixed his
eyes on them. Greatly wondering, Rama passed the
night there with his wife and brother, and at dawn
visited Chandrasekhara in the company of the well-
wishing Muni who, on arriving there, went into the
spring, and facing the sun chanted the two-lettered
mantra.

64-66.—Then, leaving Rama at the place, there
stepped into the spring Sita, the primitive energy, the
revealer of the seat of Brahma, adored by Anan-
ta and other gods, blue as a cloud, ever complacent,
three-eyed, red-lipped and fair-haired, her form glowing with fire, adorned with eight hands, and surrounded with banner and chámara (yak-tail).

रत्युक्ता तं मुनिवरः परस्मरं विद्याडयेत् ।
उविला रजनीमेका रामचन्द्रोऽतिविस्मृतः ॥ ६१ ॥
प्रभातायाम् प्रवैयाद् आह्णायासमन्वितः ।
ययौ चौचन्द्रमेश्वरं मुनिना परमेछिना ॥ ६१ ॥
सस्या मुनिवरेख्व कुण्डमध्ये ववजिताः ।
हृद्योभिमुखमाकाय जपन्मन्त्रत घ्रावरम् ॥ ६१ ॥
राज्ञं विचाय सा सीता कुण्डमध्ये ववजिता ।
चौक्षजीकृतवक्षात्रा भुजाष्टपरिशोभिता ॥ ६५ ॥
केशावचन्मिनी देवी चवरावरचन्मिनी ।
चीचलचवचंमुक्ता धवचावनरवेछिता ॥ ६५ ॥
वनमादिभिरारात्रा ब्रह्मपीठप्रकाशिका ।
चादिमसिः उपचत्रा नवावाह्वरपिनी ॥ ६६ ॥

67.—Standing on the margin, Rama saw Sita immersed in the spring. Believing the spring to have destroyed her, dear to him as life, he addressed these words to the Muni:

68-9.—"This spring shall remain in existence for the first four thousand years of the Kali age, and shall after that time vanish from the sight of man. Whoever out of devotion will drink the water, shall obtain the same fruit as may be got by immersion, and shall not live any longer upon earth."

70-71.—Saying this, the foe of Rávana went to the Mani hill. Having viewed the linga and bathed in the Lavanákbya, he gratified the sage with humble and respectful words, and then returned to Chandrasekhara.

मठखो रावयः पश्चात् सीता कुञ्जिनिवासिनी ।
अब मावयंर् कुर्वं विभाव रघुनन्दनः । ८० ॥
वक्षात्र तं मुनिवरमिदं वचनमब्रवीत् ।
कलीयत्परवादि वर्मावि कवचायतम् । ८८ ॥
जिनं कुर्वं नुसलाबीन् मानवादर्शनं भवेत् ।
भक्ति क्ला तु सीताभाः यः कविता अवं पिवेत् । ८८ ।
कुखवालावचं प्राय न पुनर्वसेवे भुमि ।
रत्युक्लाबी रावयारिर्मविपर्वतमूर्वनि । ७० ॥
अब्ला तुं दा दिवकिब कवचावी निनाज्ञावन् ।
वामय चन्द्रसेवरं प्रवाय मुनिलीवरं ।
कनाहजनवामाय रामोऽपि विनयान्विता । ७९ ॥

72.—Then Rama, delighted, started with Sita and his brother, for the banks of the Godávarí.

According to the above account, Rama, having visited the hermitage of S'arabhanga, by his direction turned towards a north-eastern city, where another sage informed him, that on the south-west of that city, there was a sacred spring of the name of his consort Sita (Sitakund), who, he was informed to his surprise, was no other than Yoganidra herself. Rama is then said to have visited this spring in the company of his wife and brother and the learned sage. Finding Sita immersed in the spring, whither she had gone to bathe without his knowledge, Rama thought she had been drowned, and cursed the spring as the destroyer of the princess. According to the malediction which, be it observed, is not to have immediate effect, the spring would cease to be visible to human eyes, at the end of four thousand years of the fourth age. The *Chinnamasti Tantra* is, however, ready with another explanation of the origin of the shrine and of its disappearance.* It

सीतामादाय यथाता भिज्ञाङ्गनयोपमा ।
जगाम परमाह्लादः पुननौदावरी प्रति ॥ ७९ ॥
दमि देवीपुराये यैयलायाम्या यच्चिकायचे खियेरयञ्जयचे
सीनीयचम्जेयमाचिरदादखीध्याया ।

* सीतागाधिकर्म कुचं पातायं कुच्चमुचलं ॥
सीतापरोचयायीय तम्बैंजदि चचार च ।
गतः सघाप छा सीता परीचाजछतापिता ॥

relates that the spring was the scene of the ordeal
by fire of Sita, that it was excavated by the hand
of the great Hanumat, and that it was cursed by
Sita herself as the site of her sufferings. The
explanation itself is, however, less important than
the manner of its narration. Sita is not described
there merely as Yoganidrá herself, or the Primeval
Sakti or Energy, and Rama the divine hero who
would curb the pride of the Rakshasas. They are
the veritable Supreme Duad, the spiritual guides of
Siva and his consort who came over to the shrine
to offer their oblations. The spiritual guide, according to Hindoo ideas, it is well known, is the embodi-
ment of the Deity itself on earth. The recognition
accordingly of Rama and Sita as the spiritual guides
of Siva and his consort is significant. A tradition
has been mentioned above, which attributes the
filling up of the spring to a dispute between the
Sivaites and Vishnuvites. It would therefore seem,
that this second legend was probably written at a
period of Vishnuvite supremacy.

एषाक्षेनाश्चिक्षे एषं दद्माचे लेन यश्चिना ।
सीताक्कापानक्षेा यच कुच्चमाच विषचर्थ ॥

* * * * * * ,

एलेन लिर्मिंतं कुच्च एरीकार्थं चमूयता ।
कुच्चपाचीचरो भूत्रा तिष्ठति चलुमान् चक्षी ॥
इति विष्णुमद्याालन्ने अवाकाष्ठीलब्याते पार्व्वतीलम्भपत्व
ज्ञालानिर्व्वेश जाम हितीचः पचक्षा ।

However it may have been, apart from the con-
tradictory nature of the two accounts which in itself
furnishes a strong argument against their authenti-
city, both of them—internally incoherent and con-
tradictory as they are—have not the impress of the
high authority of Valmiki, the most ancient writer
on the life and deeds of Rama, and perhaps the one,
who in consequence describes them with the nearest
approach to truth.   It is true that a few places in
the Chittagong Division bear the name of Rama,
so that it might apparently seem that the prince
had something or other to do with them.   There is,
for instance, Ramoo, where it is said Rama com-
menced the Setubandha bridge, but, preferring
not to enter by the postern gate the capital of
Ravana (to which the bridge would have led him, had
he gone that way), he turned round, and constructed
a separate bridge at Ramesvara to lead him to the
front gate of the metropolis of Ceylon.   In the *Pátál
Puri* (*lit.* the nether world), in a cavern in the hill of
Chandranath to which reference will presently be
made, a huge stone is pointed out as the cooking
utensil of Sita.   Similarly, a place or two in the
adjoining districts of Noakhally and the Hill Tracts,
may be mentioned as bearing the name of Rama
and his wife.   This reason, however, does not com-
mend itself as very conclusive.   For it is a fact that
may be well established by numerous instances, that
the Brahmins took delight in associating shrines

with renowned names in their religious history, in order to ensure and enhance their sanctity.* Regarding Rama alone, thus we read of the Doobrajpore rocks far off in the district of Beerbhoom, consisting of stones that fell off from his aerial chariot on his return from the Himalayas, when he had gone up there to fetch stones for the construction of his bridge to Ceylon. Adjacent places are shown, as where his wife Sita sat and bathed. A boulder in the neighbourhood is also pointed out, as having been caused by Ravana's attending a call of nature.† In the same way, Rama's advent is also claimed for the province of Orissa, (wrongly identifying it with *Kishkindhyá* mentioned in the Ramayana), where the Rajah of Cuttack up to this time wears a tail in all public receptions, more as a testimony to his descent from the monkey allies of the great hero, than by way of vindication of Mr. Darwin's theory. There are

* "The hot springs of India have attracted the notice of many observers. In the majority of instances these remarkable outbursts of water, at a temperature considerably above that of the waters, or even of the atmosphere in the neighbourhood, often charged with various gases and emitting strong odours, have been endowed by the superstitious and ignorant with wondrous virtues, or have been supposed to be the result of some miraculous interposition of divine energy." Dr Oldham on the Thermal Springs of India, page 1, Part II, Vol. XIX Memoirs of the Geological Survey of India.

† A List of the Objects of Antiquarian Interest in the Lower Provinces of Bengal compiled at the Bengal Secretariat under the orders of the Government of India, pages 4-6.

several places bearing the name of King Báli, the
brother of Sugríva, who was treacherously killed by
Rama; *Bálikáti*, a river; *Bálikánta*, also a river;
Bálisahi, a village. There is also a festival called
Báli Játrá. The *Sabdakalpadruma* also mentions
a hill at the place called *Kishkindhya*.* Against this
identification—plausible as it is—is the unfortunate
situation of the river Pampá (in Mysore) which Rama
is said to have visited, before entering *Kishkindhyá* the
kingdom of the monkeys which, it would seem, coin-
cided nearly with the present kingdom of Mysore.

It is not improbable, therefore, that the above
legends of Sitakund are another of those religio-
historical forgeries so common all over India.
Certain it is, that Rama's journey southwards
was made through the middle of the Deocan and
not through Orissa and the Coasts, much less
through Chittagong and Sitakund; the following
being the most important places in the hero's
itinerary as described by Valmiki: the Tamasá,
the Vedasruti, the Gomati, the Ganges, Batsyadesa,
Prayága, Chitrakuta, the Mandákini, Dandaka, the
Godavari, Krauncha, the Pampa, Rishyamuka,
Kishkindhya, and Ceylon. There is absolutely no
mention, in the great epic of Valmiki, of Rama
having gone so far north-eastward as Chittagong,
after having visited the hermitage of Sarabhanga.

* विचित्रन्ना चु चायुरेचन्तयन्तनविनेना । Sabdakalpadruma,
p. 679, Vol. I.

The narrative of this visit is contained in Canto V of Book III. When Rama was about to enter the hermitage of this sage, he saw with the Rishi, Indra the Dreaded Thunderer, in all the paraphernalia of his high office, who disappeared on Rama's nearer approach. Replying to Rama's question, the Muni said that the lord of heaven had been to his hermitage to escort him to heaven, but that the Muni could not comply with his request and leave the earth, before seeing Rama, to whom he offered all the merits of his long penance so that the prince by virtue of them might ascend to heaven. Rama, of course, declined the gift, and requested the sage to point out a meet place for his home. The following is his reply:

" Sutíkshna's woodland home is near,
A glorious saint of life austere,
True to the path of duty; he
With highest bliss will prosper thee.
Against the stream thy course must be
Of this fair brook Mandákiní,
Whereon light rafts like blossoms glide ;
Then to his cottage turn aside.
There lies thy path, but, ere thou go,
Look on me, dear one, till I throw
Aside this mould that girds me in
As casts the snake his withered skin.*"

* Griffith's Ramayana, Vol III, Book III, Canto V, Page 21.

On the sage giving up the ghost, the holy men who dwelt around flocked to Rama, and solicited his protection against the Rakshasas, which he readily granted. We now come to the Seventh Canto in which Rama is then made to visit this hermitage of Sutíkshna. After the exchange of proper greeting, Rama said :

"But now O saint, I pray thee tell
Where I within this wood may dwell,
For I by Sarabhanga old
The son of Gotama, was told
That thou in every lore art wise
And seest all with thy loving eyes."[*]

In reply to this, the sage begged Rama to take up his abode at his hermitage. Rama passed the night there. On the following morning he asked leave of the sage, and prayed for his permission to explore the Dandaka. The sage answered as follows :

"Go with thy brother, Rama, go,
Pursue thy path untouched by woe :
Go with thy faithful Sita, she
Still like a shadow follows thee.
Roam Dandak wood observing well
The pleasant homes where hermits dwell,
Pure saints whose ordered souls adhere
To penance rites and vows austere."[†]

---

[*] Griffith's Ramayana, Vol III, Book III, Canto VII, Page 28.
[†] Griffith's Ramayana, Vol. III, Book III, Canto VIII, Page 32.

Thus it is clear, that there is no mention whatever in the *Ramayana*, of Rama having passed through Chittagong on his way downwards to the Deccan. The geographical position itself of Chittagong and of the Godavari (to the banks of which Rama in the above legend is said to have bent his way on leaving Chittagong), renders it quite improbable. The attribution of the ordeal by fire of Sita to a hotspring is not a new idea.* The Sitakund of Monghyr is similarly credited with being the scene of the same ordeal, which, it is scarcely necessary to say, really took place at Ceylon, if the father of Aryan poetry is to be believed. The principle of human nature which led to this religious fabrication, is not, however, inexplicable. " I think it is in Macedon," reasoned Fluellen,† "where Alexander is porn. I tell you captain,—if you look in the maps of the 'orld, I warrant, you sall find in the comparisons petween Macedon and Monmouth, that the situations, look you, is poth like. There is a river in Macedon; and there is also moreover a river at Monmouth;

* In p. 209, Part I, Vol. XVII of the Journal of the Asiatic Society of Bengal, General Cunningham mentions a spring called Sitakund in Kolat, which is nine miles from Dwara, and five from Monali. In Mr. Duncan's account of the Travels in Ceylon, of a Fakeer named Pram Poory (p. 39, Vol. V of the Asiatic Researches), it is stated that "our traveller states that leaving this tank, he proceeded on to a station called *Seetakund*, where Rama placed his wife Seeta on the occasion of his war with her ravisher Ravan."

† Shakespeare, King Henry V, Act IV, Scene VII.

it is called Wye at Monmouth; put it is out of my prains, what is the name of the other river; put it is all one, 'tis alike as my fingers is to my fingers, and there is salmons in both."

It is not a little remarkable, that Sitakund, the name of a spring which, no matter whether it existed or not, now exists no longer, should (*lucus a non lucendo*) give its name to the outpost, and surpass the surrounding shrines in fame. Perhaps during a period of temporary Vishnuvite supremacy, it may have been indiscriminately used for, and may have eventually supplanted, *Panchakrosa* which, according to the sacred books, contain all the holy shrines of the place. Like the *Panchakrosi* of Benares, it stretches over 5 kroses (or 10 miles) round the village of Sitakund, being bounded* on the east by the Mandakini, on the west by Vyasakunda, on the south by Bárabakunda and on the north by the Champaka Forest. "This land called Panchakrosa," said Vishnu,† "is the cause of the holy Nirvana. Many a

* पश्चिमे व्यासकुण्डस्य पूर्वे मन्दाकिनी कुला ।
  उत्तरे चम्पकारण्ये दक्षिणे वाकुगावीहः ॥
  एतत् क्षेत्रं मया प्रोक्तं पञ्चक्रोशं महाफलं ।
  इति नारायणीतन्त्रे नारायणीजारायणसंवादे पञ्चक्रोश-
  वर्णना नाम षष्ठः पटलः ।   ‎ ‎ ‎ ‎   ‎ ‎ ‎ ‎ ‎ ‎ ‎ ‎ ‎ ‎ ‎ ‎ ‎ 'y

† पञ्चक्रोशमिदं प्रोक्तं शिवनिर्वाणकारणं ।
  एतज्जिज्ञासरे यान्ति कुत्रान्यत्रापि सर्वदा ।
  दुर्लभ्यापि भवत्येनं नम श्रीतिकरादि च ॥
                                          Ibid.

spring is contained in it, most sacred and delightful
to me." By far the most frequented of these shrines
are Vyásakunda, Bárabakunda, Lavanákhya, and the
temples of Chandranath and S'ambhunath.

The following account is given in the *Devipurana**
of the origin of the shrines of Chandranath and of
Vyasakunda.

26-27.—"Do thou tell us, O chief of the Brahmins,"
said the Rishis, " why Siva, forsaking Kasi and Kailas,
resides here in secrecy ? Why he said, 'I shall dwell
on the mount of Chandrasekhara in the Kali Yuga ;'
and why thy preceptor remains there, abandoning
all else ?"

28-29.—" In days of yore," the Suta replied, " seeing the three worlds animate and inanimate, pervaded
by the sea of curd, and immersed in the waters of
causation, the three-eyed lordly spirit created Brahmá and Vishnu for the purposes of creation.

* ऋषय ऊचुः ।

यद् विप्रेन्द्र तस्मार्थं कथं मूकमवागतः ।
विहाय काशीं कैलाशं कस्मात् गौप्यमरूपतः ॥ २६ ॥
कस्तो निवासि रत्युग्रौ गौप्यमसेखरे वने ।
कस्मात् गुरुस्तनीय याद्येन्यात् षवस्तं त्यजन् ॥ २७ ॥

सूत उवाच ।

पुरा त्रिविधविधेन त्रायं त्रिभुवनं चरं ।
क्षारदधिक्षिवे मग्नं सकारणे उपरात्वरएषु ॥ २८ ॥
दृष्टा तथाविधं सर्वं अजमानुं भूतभावनः ।
सृष्टर्थे ब्रह्मविष्णू च सृष्टार्थं त्र्यम्बकः अयात् ॥ २९ ॥

4

30-31.—"Thus created, they, infatuated with vanity, considered themselves supreme, and genitor even of the womb from which they themselves had sprung. Even in his very presence they spoke slightingly of him. Then the god, disappearing, became an image óf light.

32-35.—"From the sky he then addressed the ignorant gods thus : ' O lotus-born, of the thirteen lingas planted in Kási and other places, I have spoken to you of twelve. Only one I have concealed from thee. During the Kali Yuga, O lotus-born, I shall dwell there with Párvatí. There is no doubt of this. Do thou follow us thither with the never-dying gods.' Thus saying, Siva with Umá vanished from their sight, and went to that place.

सृष्टा तौ तस्य मिथडेऽइहारेन विमोपितौ ।
ऊतवनीं जन्मेच वदारो तौ वधूसतुः ॥ २० ॥
अत्यनीं तस्य प्रभुवे ततः वोऽपि न द्याने ।
वक्तपिंना तद्या वोऽपि ज्योतिर्लिंङं तदाभवन् ॥ २१ ॥
वब्रालावनीं तत् तौ च उवाच गमनविज्ञतः ।
येषु येषु च खानेषु मज्जिनं स्थापितं मया ॥ २२ ॥
नयीद्वद्विभागेन काश्यादिषु च पग्रज ।
द्वाद्श कविलं तुर्थ द्विगलेवं जुतोप च ॥ २३ ॥
वक्तो गिद्यामि नवीन पार्वत्या नाप चंबकः ।
पूर्व वच्चन तेऽवेव गभिषेधेष्यमु तप च ॥ २४ ॥
गभिषाच ततः पश्चाद्समरेण्य पग्रज ।
दग्युङ्गाजापितः मभुद्यवावाद्य उमवा उप ॥ २५ ॥

86-87.—Even now the linga may be seen there, called Haragauri. The sinless place remained very secret in the first three ages. For the weal of men, the bull-drawn god dwells in the Kali Yuga in that sacred place with the never-dying ones."

Having thus premised the presence in the sacred place, of Siva and his consort, of Brahmá, Vishnu, and other gods, the story then runs as follows:

88.—Once on a time Vyasa, the son of Parás'ara, the subduer of his passions, began to practise asceticism in the company of the wise residents of *Kasi* (Benares), full of beatitude, knowing the Supreme Spirit, and wearing matted hair.

89-42.—Seeing him the son of Matsyagandhá, of unknown lineage, caste, and character, seated with

क्वापि हरते तिहैं परलोरैति बैधकम् ।
तत् बियुगे बातिमुपैं बाबीबोबैब बाबबं ॥ १६ ॥
ततो प्रकामरूपेब बोकाबाबु बिलाब वै ।
एबद्देवामरैबीर्बे बबबं (?) नं ह्बाद्वमद् ॥ १७ ॥
एकदा बाब्देबेंऽपि काबीचेबबिबाबिबिभिः ।
तपः कर्तुब् समारेले पाराबर्यां. पर्त्तयः ॥ १८ ॥
मबाबन्द्बिमप्रैनैकामव्वक्वभारिभिः ।
तपबा मौलकबुर्षः ब्बब्बिब्रिविनेकिभिः ॥ १९ ॥
बिबब्बानान्बुबिः बर्बं ब्राबितं अब्माबिकम् ।
तब्रा तीबे मबाबार्बं बाराबब्बिबाबर्बम् ॥ ४० ॥
बातिमौकुबिबीबें तं मब्बगन्बाबबं मुबिं ।
एबाब्बबद्माबाबाद्व एकबेब-बिबाबिबबुं ॥ ४१ ॥
हुक्षीबं बब्ब तब्ब मुबौबाबिब तिब्रक्ब्वम् ।
बिबब्ले च मबा बौबी बाबाब बेबबाबिबिभिः ॥ ४२ ॥

themselves on the same seat, and dwelling in the
same holy place, although he was very wise, the
ornament of the sages, like unto Vishnu himself, the
ire of the holy dwellers was roused against Vyasa.

43-44.—Full of jealousy, Bhrigu addressed to him
the following words : "Who art thou ? Whence dost
thou come ? Whose son and of what family art
thou ? Where didst thou formerly dwell ? Speak
the truth."

45-46.—Vyasa replied : "I am the son of Parasara by Matsyagandhá. I have come here to see you,
and to worship the god Visvanath. I would dwell
with you, O sages of good actions. Let a seat
amongst you be granted to me."

47-48.—While he was thus speaking, Vyasa was
interrupted by Bhrigu with these angry and unseemly
words : "Hear, O ye Munis, the account of his

सर्वो अनुपतिखन्तु ग्रोवाचेखोपुतं नयः । ४२ ॥

अनुरुवाच ।

बक्तम् क्रम रुयायातः कस्य खरुः कुत्तव किद् ।
कस्मिन्निवसतिः पूर्वं यद एतर्थ नयन्य जा ॥ ४४ ॥

व्यास उवाच ।

वराशरसुतोऽवद्‌ वे मत्स्यगन्धोदरीङ्गवः ।
युष्मान् मद्रु रुवावानी विष्वनावख सेवना ॥ ४५ ॥
पुच्छाभिषु रुवावारं करोमि मुनिपुङ्गवाः ।
साधुभिः क्तनकर्मीभिर्दीयतां खिन्निवनखमा ॥ ४६ ॥
तत्रेव वाचमानखु मयोभिषु उनम्भितः ।
निरस्तो अमुचा बाचः कामत्रोधविवर्द्धितः ॥ ४७ ॥
मत्सगमश्राद्धतकं वि प्रसु याचः कुखोजभ्मितः ।
शंयुषं मुनयः सर्वो यख आखमदीतनद् ॥ ४८ ॥

birth, and thou too, the son of Matsyagandhí, the disgrace of thy family, listen to my words.

49-58.—"While thy mother, begotten of a fish and with a fishy smell, was a ferry-woman in the Jumna, Parasara one day came to the bank of the river and entered her boat. To the Muni's sight she immediately appeared to be endowed with beauty and grace, breathing perfume, a soul-ravishing maid of sixteen. Seeing her, the Muni became full of desire. Thou art the offspring of this union, and art neither a Kunda, nor a Golaka. How canst thou presume to practise asceticism with us? Go to thy own proper place. Thou shouldst not tarry here for a moment."

54-56.—Hearing these insulting words, Vyasa, the son of Satyavati and Parasara, being irate, thought of sacrificing himself to Siva (thus making Siva

यदा मे अजनी पाषीत् यमुनार्था चरिचरी ।
मौनजागात् बन्धुता तरवौष्टरीमा घमी ॥ ४८ ॥
देवात् परामरखन चामय यमुनातटं ।
चारख्रा तरवौं सख्या मुनेर्मैगलः चयात् ॥ ४० ॥
चुलाखा चुरखा शांति बहुलातिमलोरमा ।
एजस्था षोकुमाद्वीया रूपकान्तञ्चसंयुता ॥ ४१ ॥
उद्गा तां चच कामाख्रो रतिमघ्रः ततखया ।
तनीन्द्रवीरस्ति चा प्राङ्गः न कुन्ता न च गोषकः ॥ ४२ ॥
षोऽज्ञाभिक्षं मया कर्तुं मन्त्रोचि कचलप च ।
मत्मार्थं तव जनकार्ण न चेषे चचलप च ॥ ४३ ॥
मुना परामरचुनी चचखदातमचिम्बलम् ।
वर्ष चिवाय दाखामि चेत्वौदयं चिभाव च ॥ ४४ ॥

guilty of his death), and said, "O vile and false Siva, holder of the trident, blue-throated, and hide-garmented, why dost thou appear *Asiva* or in-auspicious to me? Why dost thou harass me so often? This very day I will leave this place."

57.—When he the subduer of his passions was so minded, the bull-drawn and blue-throated god made himself manifest to him the chief of the wise men, and spoke as follows:

58-60.—"Certes thou art a portion of mine, O sub-duer of thy passions, and learned in the cause of things. There is a seat of mine on Mount Chandra-sekhara, very secret, and unattainable even by the gods. There in Chandrasekhara I will always reside in the Kali Yuga with Uma.

चरो द्विषाषियं से च वर्तते मूद्रश्वक पुरा ।
कच्च विच्रमणं से वे मौच्चकच्छाजिलाम्बर ॥ ५५ ॥
रतो मच्छामि चर्चैव पामराच्चानयच्चक ।
चमर्षाविद रत्युक्षा वाषः चम्यवमीहृतः ॥ ५६ ॥
वेषाद्धिर्षंद्रा ममुच्च ममच्छामे परचमयः ।
तदा द्याच्चकः षाच्चाद्यभवत् तच्च पूर्षतः ॥ ५० ॥
उवाच मं स्वामिवरं मौच्चकच्छो द्यच्चमजः ।
म चन्देशो मदंमक्षयु प्रधु माषं परचमप ॥ ५८ ॥
वेषं मेऽ्लीष मुच्चं मत्ु देवाचामपि दुर्लभ्यं ।
मवाराष्ठं मवानुच्चं मौच्चमहेवरं मुमे ॥ ५८ ॥
रैवाभिह्मिषितं वेषं काचिष्कीदेऽच्छि मच्चमित् ।
चदा चष्टो च चाच्चामि चमवा चन्द्रहेवरे ॥ ६० ॥

61-68.—" Know, O Sage, that Chandrasekhara sur-
passes all other sacred places. It is covered on all
sides with branches of trees, which protect it from
the sun and rain. The *kokilas* sing there with sweet
voice. In the recesses of the forest dwell the
sages, their looks probing the Inmost Cause of the
universe; Brahmá and other gods bathe there day
and night; and in the hermitages dwell the Rishis,
Yakshas, Gandharvas, and Bhairavas. In that forest
are trees with flowers and fruits of the six seasons. The forest itself is in one place very deep and
secret, and in another place rocky, like the moon half-
eclipsed. On the south-west of the forest, O subduer of thy passions, is the Sindhu (the Ocean), the
King of all *tirthas*, to whose embrace the sacred

सर्वेषेपाधिकं विद्धि श्रीचन्द्रशेखरं मुने ।
सर्वेषां कुसुमाद्याभिज्छादितं वारिताानां ॥ ६१ ॥
वनप्रियादिभिस्तप कूजितं मधुरैः खरैः ।
ज्ञानिभिस्तपवद्देव शोधवे नववाकरे ॥ ६२ ॥
तप ब्रह्मादिभिस्तप खानं चस्मे जवर्विनं ।
ब्रवयप घनमयनी यत्राच मैदवाखथा ॥ ६३ ॥
छिद्रा मचर्मेयी वप नितमाचम् तदाखसे ।
भङ्कतु-फलपुषादिः पादपाः षन्ति मघने ॥ ६४ ॥
वमकामजातिमुल्ल वनं सर्वतुं मनोभवं ।
चन्ये जनविधेने पतू मलाघमार्षचन्द्रवत् ॥ ६५ ॥
तचा दचिवतः सिन्धुचीर्वेराजः परन्तप ।
वचा षंखोमावाता मचा भागीरथी द्विज ॥ ६६ ॥
वचा चिमाचिने स्वाखा मचा श्रीचन्द्रशेखरः ।
श्रीचन्द्रशेखरे देवैः षदा आख्यामि वे मुने ॥ ६७ ॥

Ganga offers herself, led by Bhagiratha. As the Himalaya is dear to me, so is Chandrasekhara. There shall I, O Muni, dwell with the gods."

Thus instructing Vyasa, the god then made himself manifest to him in his own proper form which is described at length in the text.

74–78.—" In his own form, O Munis, he then said to Vyasa : " Go there, O most excellent of sages, subduer of thy passions, where I shall dwell with Uma. Thou shalt attain all thy desires ; have no doubt about thy success. That seat of mine is the giver of health and wealth, and after death, of salvation. There also dwells the rice-giving Annapurna, delighting in rice and nectar. In this seat of perfection shall I dwell, the lord of Parvati." Saying this to the Muni, the god disappeared.

जल्लोपरिवं मकि व व नभूव परजयः ।
ग्रवअतिवऋमंन्तुप्रमिमः क्रपवौल्लज्जः ॥ १८ ॥
* * * * * * * *
* * * * * * * *

रमीः कपविमेवेषु भगवानुमवा ७ष ।
वषामि मय रत्युक्ते बाचाय मुमिगुङ्मवा ॥ ७४ ॥
मत्र गच्छ मुमिमेत मकिग्रमे परजय ।
वद्गमीष प्राप्स्यमि ये मु षन्वं षिविमे संमवा ॥ ७५ ॥
मत्वैवं मिवरं जजलमो व मीषद्गावकम् ।
वत्रपूवों मिवषमि वद्गात्मरूपधारिवौ ॥ ७६ ॥
पन व हुंजमावे वेद्गग्रमावाविजाषिमी ।
एवभूतं षिवपीठे वषत्मय (?) पार्वतीपतिसु ॥ ७७ ॥
रास्मुज्जानादेषे वष्मा मुमवे ज्ञानमाजिमे ॥ ७८ ॥

79-81.—As Nárada had ascended the Srísaila hill, even so went Vyasa, the son of Satyavati, to Chandrasekhara, hearing these words of Siva. There he began to practise asceticism, his mind always concentrated in meditation, repeating the five-lettered mantra, sometimes covered with snow, sometimes near a fire, sometimes fasting altogether, absorbed in Pránáyáma, all his thoughts devoted to the meditation on god.

82.—Pleased at seeing him so devoted, the Self-created then appeared to him. " Ask for a boon," he said, " O subduer of thy passions."

88-85.—Having heard this, Vyasa then replied with folded hands—" When the Munis residing at Kasi spoke scornfully to me, it was by thy command O Lord, that I came here. Dwell thou here, as was thy command while in Kasi. This is the dear boon that I ask of thee."

ततः शम्भुतीर्थानुं भुक्त्वा शर्व्वं परस्य तु ।
ययौ शोभनमभेश्वरं शौभैते नारदौ यथा ॥ ७८ ॥
तत्र तपः शमारेभे तदा च ध्यानमानसः ।
विमलाछशतः ऋषिभुतामनशनीपतः ॥ ८० ॥
निरादारौ कदा देवे तह्रायभावमानतः ।
ध्यायानमानतः ऋषिम् पञ्चाचरमनुं अपत् ॥ ८१ ॥
एतं नपीरमलेचैव जतभुतमेभमानतः ।
भुत्वा प्रत्यजमवदत् वरं बृहु परमप ॥ ८२ ॥
ततः भुत्वा भगवान् बाचा शतात्मशिपुडोऽत्रबीत् ।
मर्चितं ने कदा एव मुनिभिः काशीवासिभिः ॥ ८३ ॥
नयोपदेशमाद् मनजमनपेछेन मया विभो ॥ ८४ ॥
तस्मात् यनोपदेशं ने काशीशेन मयाजमा ।

86-87.—"Do thou, O sage," the god answered, "remain on the mount Chandrasekhara near the ocean, as the guardian deity of this holy place, and make thyself the saviour of the three worlds by planting over it all the *tirthas*, such as Gaya and others, that exist on the face of the earth. May all thy desires be successful."

88-89.—With these words, the god, while yet in the presence of Vyasa, pierced the earth with his trident. Then there arose a spring full of water, with igneous brilliance in the interior, and covered with smoke.

90-93.—Delighted at this sight, Vyasa assumed the

तथा अवाच विरिंच देवि वेवं वरं सुवन् ॥ ८५ ॥
सन्नतौ चेक्षराम नौयीपिडितविषया ।
सिव विम्बलीपे च नौपन्दमेच्चरे मुने ॥ ८६ ॥
जयादीनीच नौयांनि यानि सन्तीच भूतले ।
ताभ्यच ज्ञापयित्वा तु नैवाकवतारच् कुर ॥ ८७ ॥
विविभंयु वेश्रीट्टा इत्युक्ताचे ज्ञपानिधि ।
च तथा पञ्जनाः सकृ चिन्द्रकेन विसन्वरे ॥ ८८ ॥
श्रीऽपि कृष्णात्तिमिर्लेला वारिपूर्णो बभूव च ।
तच्चाकारेऽग्निभा दीप्तिः स्रियसे भूमवेष्टिता ॥ ८९ ॥
इत्थानन्दवनो बाह्यवय पचिनता जयत् ।
परं श्रादानतया्े धमा पाषाचविपचय् ॥ ९० ॥
विभुजमुपगीतय् जडानचक्षधारिवं ।
यर्खीाम्बरदीषां कनौन्मै हेमित् जयत् ॥ ९१ ॥
यच्च भावाविकसिदच् वेदसार्वेजितं जयत् ।
वेदान्त-सचादिनु विलेख ज्ञानहचर्वेः ॥ ९२ ॥
पुनाग्य च तु वेचीर्खं धर्मीभवौरुवायकः ॥ ९३ ॥
इति देवीपुरादे वैचतासारौर जयचुरचसवामनि पचितावन्चे
खन्दबोम्नाया ।

form of stone, and became absorbed in meditation on
its west side. Even now he may be seen there, two-
handed, wearing the sacred thread, and clotted hair,
clothed in deer-skin, the expositor of virtue and
vice, who, churning the ocean of Vedic literature
with the rod of his knowledge, for the first time
explained the whole universe according to the dictum
of the Vedas. Let him purify the world."

Such was the origin of the shrine of Chandranath
and of Vyasakunda. As in the legend of Sitakund
the spring is to vanish from human sight at the end
of four thousand years of the Kali Yuga, so in this
legend also the shrines are to be manifest to human
eyes at the commencement of the same Yuga. In
both cases, great names in history have been
brought forward to father the foundation of the
shrines. Rama, it is known, is the deified hero of
the Ramayana. Vyasa, according to the late Mr.
Sherring,* has two or three temples dedicated to
him in Benares; but he is not generally considered
to be a deified hero. Nevertheless, no name is so
distinguished in the whole field of Indian history
as the name of this sage. To him is ascribed the
compilation of the Vedas and Puranas. To him
is attributed the fatherhood of the fathers of the
Kauravas and the Pándavas. It is no wonder,
therefore, that the sage should have been made to

* Sherring's Sacred City of the Hindus, p. 118.

play the part that he has been made to play in the
foregoing passage. This, however, is not the first
time, that he has been credited with the ambition of
founding a shrine. The *Annadámangala* relates
a like attempt on his part. Expelled by Siva
from Kaśi (Benares), Vyasa began to practise
extremely mortifying austerities, in the hope of rais-
ing a shrine that would, in every respect, surpass the
Kaśi of Siva. He had well nigh succeeded in his
object, when Uma, Siva's consort, one day appeared
before him in the guise of an old, deaf, and decrepit
woman, and asked him what merit a man would
acquire by dying at his *tírtha*. Vyasa replied that
the man would obtain salvation. But still the old
woman pretended not to have heard his answer,
and repeated the question again and again. Vexed
at this, Vyasa said that the man would become an
ass, who died there. Siva's consort, then assuming
her own form, said " so be it," and vanished from the
place.* The later attempt of Vyasa to found a *tírtha*
in Chittagong appears to have been more successful.
He not only succeeds in conciliating Siva, but also
obtains from him the much-desired boon. "Do thou,
O sage," the god is made to have said, "remain on

* জিজ্ঞাসিয়া কহিলা ক্রোধে কাশের কুহরে ।
পাষ্টি হইবে বুড়ী এখানে যে মরে ॥
বুঝিনু বুঝিনু বলি মরে যাতি কাশ ।
তথাত বলিয়া দেবী বৈলা অদর্শন ॥

* 'Annadámangala, p 158. This legend is based on the Kaśíkhanda
of the Skanda Purana.

the mount Chandrasekhara near the ocean, as the
guardian deity of this holy place, and make thyself the
saviour of the three worlds by planting over it all the
tirthas, such as Gaya and others, that exist on the face
of the earth. May all thy desires be successful."

The pilgrim to the shrines of Sitakund generally
takes up his quarters at the lodging-houses of the
Adhikáris, a class of Brahmins, who send out
emissaries called Pándás to almost every district of
the Lower Provinces, in order to persuade people to
undertake a pilgrimage to these shrines. These
Pándás serve as guides to the pilgrims, and, in the
shape of remuneration, get from the Adhikaris their
passage-money as well as a portion, generally the
fourth part, of their eventual gain; for the Adhikaris, besides the rent of the lodging-houses, also
receive whatever the pilgrim offers to the gods,
clothes, cows, horses, palkis, silver and gold ornaments,—the *kar* or the visiting cess, which consists
of eight annas only under the District Magistrate's
orders, being paid to the Mohunta for the mainte-
nance of the shrines. The earnings of the Adhikaris
average Rs. 5,000, and sometimes rise to Rs. 10,000.
They have now-a-days found competitors in people
of other castes, who also have set up lodging-
houses of their own. The most opulent Adhikaris
are Ramahari Adhikari, Chandrasekhara Adhikari,
Gopínath Adhikari, and Akhil Chandra Adhikari.
Hinduism is, however, at a discount in Chittagong.

The few Brahmins that may be found there, are
certainly not the ornaments of the learned class.
Some excellent rules were framed by Mr. Kirkwood,
lately Magistrate of Chittagong, for the construction
and ventilation of the lodging-houses. These, together
with a hospital erected near the local bazar, have
served to prevent the spread of disease which, in
former days, used to originate and spread around,
from the large concourse of people that assembled
at the *melas*. The Adhikaris have now to take out
licenses from the Magistrate to lodge pilgrims, which
are refused, if their lodging-houses do not conform
with the prescribed rules.

Settling himself in one of these lodging-houses,
the pilgrim proceeds to bathe in the *Vyásakunda*
referred to above. This is a small tank, 120 × 90
hands, full of mud and shrubs, the water being so
impure that one would abhor the touch of it. I was
informed that, small as the tank was, it was believed
that no one could swim across it, or throw a stone from
one side of it to the other. After bathing in the *Kunda*
which, however, does not indicate any signs of being
of an igneous nature as related in the legend trans-
lated above, the pilgrim makes offerings to the *Bata*
(*Ficus Indica*) tree, underneath which Vyasa is said to
have performed the Asvamedha sacrifice.* This tree

* ————————————यज्ञसीपना ।

॥व्याचमेधमखरोडपिविमीद्रावयं ॥

इति श्रीवाराहीतन्त्रे श्रीजारावयीनारायवयंवादे
ज्ञत्तीकाः पडड्ः ।

represents the primeval Bata tree, under which the
great Vishnu rested before the creation. It serves as
the veritable " door-keeper " of the god Chandranath,
and is the presiding deity of the plain below.*　It is
said never to grow old, and to flower in all seasons
for the worship of the god.　The pilgrim throws upon
the tree-deity clods of earth, of which it is said to
be very fond, and circumambulates it.　The temple
of Vyasa is pointed out, lying on the margin of the
spring in a very dilapidated state.

Thence the pilgrim proceeds to the temple of
S'ambhunáth, or Svayambhunáth, the Self-created
Lord.　As you proceed, the mount Chandrasekhara
appears before you in full majesty. You feel a
presence.　No wonder that they said that the gods
resided there.　Are the Munis still meditating there
on God, under the tall pine-trees? Are the gods and
nymphs disporting themselves on the hillocks?　All
the old Hindu associations force themselves on you
despite your Western education.　The feeling, however, fades away, when you come to the site of the
Sítákund mentioned above. According to the *Varahi
Tantra*† there are five Kundas at this place called

* ॐ वट्टकः वतिट्वय नन्दीमचेनानाथकः ।
　निर्विषं कुट् देवेष पयबोट्टुमियः षट्ा ॥
　वट्नाबी नयाटष्ः देवरहारणाषकः ।
　　　　इति षोवाराषीतनं षोवाराषदीनाराषदसंवाट
　　　　　　क्षीयाः पट्कः ।

† तत्ः पूर्वपवाटस्या वाछुर्वतनवषिधौ ।
　तनौष विन्छुरैवय नानदौमरष पचिमे ॥

*Sítákunda, Rámakunda, Lakshmanakunda, Brisha-
kunda and Nábhikunda.* Sítákund, as related above,
is no longer in existence. Small holes are, however,
pointed out as the other Kundas. Near them, in
an old temple are the images of Ráma, Sítá, and
Lakshmana. These are stone figures, very awkwardly
done, unlike the graceful idols of Calcutta.

Jyotirmaya consists of flickering tongues of volcanic flames in the right side of the ascent to the
temple of S'ambhunath. The flames, it is said, dis-
appear altogether at the touch of the impious.
When we visited Jyotirmaya, we found that it had
been completely put out; and it was not till the
Mohunta of Sitakund, who was acting as our *cicerone*,
brought another light in contact with it, that the
tongues could be lighted again. It is said that the
flames move about from place to place, sometimes
appearing in the temple of S'ambhunath, sometimes
in other places, and at times burn a whole forest.

पञ्चकुण्डान्वितं खानं परमं ब्रह्मदायकम् ।
इन्द्रकुर्षे परं यत्र ब्राह्मं ब्योतीश्वराख्यकम् ॥
ग्रतः ब्रह्मादयः सुरा नित्यं निवन्ति चानले ।
पातालादुद्भिता देवी गङ्गा तत्पूर्वसा ग्रमात् ॥
नञ्जनं ग्रर्वमादेवि सर्वपापात् प्रमुच्यते ।
नब्योतीरत्नेश्वरं ग्राभिमुखं ग्रमीश्वरम् ॥
नब्योतीरत्नमङ्गार्घं (?) रामकुर्षे ग्रमीश्वरम् ।
वद्भवत्स नवोदीर्घं सीतायाः कुण्डमुत्तमम् ॥
                   इति श्रीवाराहीतन्त्रे श्रीवाराघवजराघवौ-
                   ग्रवादे चतुर्थं पटलः ।

The Mohunta told us that, on one occasion when he was coming down from the temple of Chandranath, he was overtaken and scorched by the flames which suddenly appeared in great force, on the way between him and the temple of S'ambhunath. When we visited Chandrasekhara, we found that a considerable portion of the forest on both sides of our way, had been recently burnt down by the fire. Some portion or other of the range of mountains always exhibits traces of the flames. At night, we witnessed an extensive conflagration on a distant hillock. Lord Teignmouth was probably referring to Jyotirmaya, when he wrote the following: "On the side of a hill distant about three miles from the burning well (Barabakunda), there is a spot of ground, of a few feet only in dimensions, from which flashes of fire burst on stamping strongly with the foot. The appearance of this spot resembled that of earth on which a fire had been kindled. I do not recollect whether it was hot to the touch."[*]

The linga S'ambhunáth, the self-created lord, is said to form part of the body of the hill. A tradition is told that one of the kings of Tipperah made great endeavours to dig it out from the shrine, in order to carry it over to his capital, but without success. He was directed, it is added, by the god to content himself with the goddess Tripurásundarí, whom he accordingly took over to his kingdom.

* Lord Teignmouth's Memoirs of Sir William Jones, Vol II. p. 68.

In the history of Tipperah written by Baboo Kailas
Chandra Sinha,[*] we certainly read of king Kumára
having gone to visit a linga in Syámalanagar, which
the historian considers to be identical with Chittagong. We also read of his grandson king
Taksharao, who was a devout worshipper of Siva,
but had failed to obtain a son through the in-
fluence of the god, having wounded the god in his
feet. Offended at this treatment, the god is said to
have left Tipperah. But it is also related that king
Taksharao then propitiated the irate god with a
human sacrifice, and got two sons by his influ-
ence. It is not impossible, that this statement
may have connexion with the attempt to transplant
the linga S'ambhunáth; but an old officer belonging
to the Chittagong Collectorate informed me, that the
belief that the linga formed part of the body of the
mount, was groundless,—it being a movable stone
having artificially imprinted on it in wax the marks
of natural lingahood[†]—and that the temple was pur-
posely kept dark to avoid detection. Mr. Casperaz,
the Assistant Magistrate, who was deputed in 1879
to superintend the *Siva Chaturdasí* mela, proposed

---

[*] Babu Kailas Chandra Sinha's Chronicles of Tipperah, p. 5.

[†] नानाशिङ्ग्रहमायुक्तं नानावर्णसमन्वितम् ।
वारहमूर्त पठितं सर्वत्र भुवि सम्मते ।
मणिमत्रु सधभूतमपरं सनवसुनम् ॥

इति शिवागमेश्वरः ।

Vide p. 257 of the *Pránatoshiní.*

to the District Magistrate the opening of an aperture in the dome, to serve as a skylight which would prevent people from looking in, as well as give light and air. The well-meant suggestion could not, I believe, be carried out, as it was necessary to avoid what might have been misunderstood as uncalled for interference on the part of Government. The temple of S'ambhunáth was erected down below in the plateau of the hill, as the ascent to that of Chandranath is not practicable throughout the year, especially in the rainy season which is somewhat long in that part of the country, owing to its being hilly. It consists of two apartments. In the outer apartment are the Bhairava, Rama, Sita, Lakshmana, Hanumat, Annapurná and others. The presiding deity is in the inner apartment, and is of course, very superior. "The sight of the face of Kramadísa (another name of S'ambhunáth) saves one from future birth."* The linga is of a cylindrical form, about four inches in diameter, and rising about five inches from a cone, the base of which has been walled around.

In the court-yard of the main temple of S'ambhunáth are many minor shrines crumbling to decay. There is a temple of *Káli*, the dread consort of

---

* अमरीमलुषं दृष्टा पुनर्जन्म न विद्यते ।
इति चौवाराचीतमे नारायणीनारावबर्षवादे
वन्मचेश्वरवर्षेजा सारं नष्टः पठन्ता ।

Siva; a mandir of *Jagannáth*, and *Rádhá Krishna*;
and *mount Govardhana* so well known in Brindávana.
Close by are the eight Bhairavas, and the burial places
of some of the Mohuntas of Sitakund. On the left,
after passing S'ambhunáth, is a sacred spring with
pucca sides called *Gyákunda*,—which is considered
equal in merit to the famous shrine at Gaya,—where
the pilgrim shaves and bathes, and offers oblations
to the manes of his ancestors. Proceeding upwards,
the path becomes a mere track, with no attempt at
being a regular road such as leads up to S'ambhunath. We now come to the base of mount *Chandrasekhara.* The grand staircase—consisting of about
575 steps, and generally supposed to have been
built by one of the kings of Tipperah,—which brings
the pilgrim to the temple of *Chandranáth* at the top
of the Chandrasekhara hill, is giving way a little
here and there; and unless repaired in time, will
render the ascent more difficult in future than in
the days before their construction. Chandrasekhara* is the highest peak in Chittagong, being
1155 feet in height, and is situate in the centre of
the Sitakund range which, commencing from the

* Chandranáth is the name of the god. The peak is called
Chandrasekhara. It is also sometimes called Chandranáth. Dr.
Hunter also calls it Chandinath. Although Chandinath is another
name of Siva, I have never heard the hill called by that name. It
is, however, usual to use Chandranath and Sitakund as synonymous
terms.

northern end of the Sudder station of the district,
runs without interruption to Tipperah, parallel to
the Grand Trunk Road. In the *Nirvána-tantra** it is
mentioned as one of the *Kulaparvatas* or principal
mountains of India. Wilson in his Dictionary erro-
neously places it in Arracan. "In the hill of Sitakund there is a stone of two descriptions, one apparently of volcanic formation, and porous, the other
solid containing iron." The hill is "formed of a
stratum inclined at an angle of 30° north-east and
south-west, of hard clay in places; and in others of
sandstone. The surface is generally covered with
loam, but on the southern slopes of all the outskirting
hills, it is red sandstone or sand.†" The original
temple on this peak, built by a king of Tipperah, fell
down in the cyclone of 1848, when the present
structure, which is of smaller dimensions, was erected by Ram Sundar Sen, a rich merchant, who has
since fallen from his high estate. The temple has
little pretensions to artistic beauty. But the view
around the peak was exceedingly beautiful. A ship
that was sailing far off in the Bay of Bengal, appeared like a bird slowly flying on the horizon. The

* नीलाचले मन्दरख पर्वतं चन्द्रभैरवम् ।
विमाचयं पुरैव्य मखयं भवपर्वतम् ।
चतुर्णोचे चवैरेषि रत्न चमञ्जकाचखम् ॥
इति निर्वाणतन्त्रे पर्वतननोपाखानमे चतुरोदि-
खमादे कैलविखरं नाम चतुर्थो पटलः ।

† Statistics of the Lower Provinces of Bengal for 1868-69, p. 26

ascent of the hill itself, it is said, gives salvation.*
The god, however, is an ordinary linga. Sitakund
was, as stated before, visited by Sir Joseph Hooker.
The following is an extract from the account given
by him in page 852 of Vol. II of his Himalayan
Journals: "The road to the top of Seetakund leads
along a most beautiful valley, and then winds up a
cliff that is in many places almost precipitous, the
ascent being partly by steps cut in the rock of which
there are 560 (?). The mountain is very sacred, and
there is a large Brahmin temple on its flank; and
near the base a perpetual flame bursts out of the
rock. This we were anxious to examine, and were
extremely disappointed to find it a small vertical
hole in a slaty rock, with a lateral one below for a
draught, and that it is daily supplied by pious pilgrims and Brahmins with such enormous quantities
of ghee (liquid butter), that it is to all intents and
purposes an artificial lamp; no trace of natural
phenomena being discoverable." I do not know to
what flame Dr. Hooker thus alludes. Jyotirmaya is
at the foot of the hill, and is also visited by pious
pilgrims. But there can be no doubt that it is a
natural phenomenon.

In order to visit *Virupáksha*, a phallic symbol of

* सौवन्नसेश्वरादीये मुक्तिमायोगि मानका ॥
रति सौभारासौतमके नारायचौनारावचवंवाये
वन्मसेश्वरवर्षेगा मास नच्चा पठका ।

Siva (similar to Chandranath and Sambhunath,
mentioned above), in a temple situated midway down
the descent from Chandrasekhara, the pilgrim de-
scends by a north-east route.   Many proceed to Chandranath after visiting Virupáksha. The ascent to
this temple from the foot of the mountain is not a
pleasant affair.   Sometimes you have to take a long
leap, holding in your hand the frail root of an old
tree. If it gives way, you are at once precipitated
into the abyss below, which seems unfathomable.
On his way to Chandranath from Virupaksha, the
pilgrim visits *Unakoti Sivalinga* in a picturesque
spot called *Pátála Puri,* or the nether world, covered
with green foliage, and full of the beauties of nature.
The undulations in the rocky surface of the cave,
drenched with water issuing from the sides of it,
are pointed out as Unakotí or 99 lacs of Sivas.
What Mr. Sherring said of its prototype in Benares
applies to this: "The actual number cut out on
the superficies of the stone is not more than a few
hundred; but the Hindoos are not particular in
their definition of numbers."* Descending from
Virupáksha, we meet the former road again at the
Mandákiní. This stream is considered to be identical with the river in heaven of the same name.
It is said that the Ganges on starting from the
Himálaya divided itself into three streams, one
running through heaven called Mandakiní, another

* Sherring's Sacred City of the Hindoos, p. 100.

flowing on earth called Gangá, and the third Bhoga-
vatí, which is in the nether world. The water of the
stream is certainly very clear, cool, and sweet.

Of the other shrines, *Bárabakunda* is a volcanic
well. It is about three miles' journey southwards
from the Sitakund village, and is situated in the
same range of hills. Báraba fire, according to ancient
mythology,* originated from the anger of the Muni
Aurva, whose mother's womb was about to be ripped
open by the Kshatriyas. It was deposited in the
bed of the sea, to prevent it from burning the
three worlds. It is stated in the *Varahí Tantra*† that
Baraba is the veritable fire which sprang from the
third eye of Siva and destroyed Káma, and that it
is to burn down the three worlds at the final annihi-
lation. The same Tantra also relates that the spring
s four cubits square, with tepid water, and th at the

* तमर्थे क्रोधसञ्जातं चौर्वौऽग्निं यदवाब्रमे ।
उन्नुधर्व्वे च चैनाप जययुक्ते मरोदधौ ॥ ११ ॥
अनबयजिरी भूमा यत्नादेवविदो विदुः ।
तमग्निमुक्तिरत्तब्रात् पिवत्यामी मरोदधिः ॥ १२ ॥
इति चौमबाहारवे चादिपर्व्वेषि पैचरचयचौ-
चौपाज्ञानेऽसौत्यभिदमतनमोऽध्याया ।
चयचिदः = चक्रचामचय् । इति भारतभामदीपाख्यभारतटीकाया मौचबचः ।

† शेतमेचानचसञ्जातौ अज्ञानमे च दुर्नेचः ।
कालौ भज च धंचौचौ चैन मेचाग्निना पुरा ॥
चिधौर्त्त रचावे चैन वमुमरेव धावौ ।
युचाले रचावे चैन मच्यार्थे चयरावच्त् ॥
चाराच्याम् उप्तमः पच्ठः ।

fire consists of seven flames.* The following account of the spring is given by Lord Teignmouth :†
" The burning well is situated about twenty-two miles
from Chatigan, at the termination of a valley surrounded by hills. I visited it in 1778, and, from
recollection, am enabled to give the following account
of it :—the shape of the well, or rather reservoir, is
oblong, about six feet by four, and the depth does
not exceed twelve feet. Tho water, which is always
cold, is supplied by a spring, and there is a conduit
for carrying off the superfluity; a part of the
surface of the well, about a fourth, is covered with
brick-work, which is nearly ignited by the flames,
which flash without intermission from the surface of
the water. It would appear that an inflammable
vapour escapes through the water, which takes fire
on contact with the external air; the perpetuity of
the flame is occasioned by the ignited brick-work
as, without this, much of the vapour would escape
without conflagration. This was proved by taking
away the covering of brick-work after the extinc-
tion of the heat, by throwing upon it the water of

* तत्र हविष्यदेवी देवि कुर्यं नाकृपर्वन्न्रवम् ।
मोचारमे विष्ववे कुर्यं चतुर्वेर्यं सुवोभानम् ॥
वम्जिन्द्राक्षकी वक्रिः नुन्निवेचरचत्रिभौ ।
तन्जवनौमङुच्यव तत्राग्निः शिवरुपिवः (?) ॥
गारान्ग्राम् उग्नक: पङ्क्ष ।

† Lord Teignmouth's Memoirs of Sir William Jones, p. 56.

the well. The flames still continued to burst forth
from the surface, but with momentary intermissions
and the vapour was always immediately kindled by
holding a candle at a small distance from the
surface of the water. A piece of silver placed in
the conduit for carrying off the superfluous water,
was discoloured in a few minutes, and an infusion
of tea gave a dark tinge to the water."

Compare with the above, Captain Pogson's description of the spring—"In front is a building about
thirty feet square, over the spring; the descent to it,
by a flight of steps, is about fifteen feet; the rising
heat was like that of a hot bath. Flames, in succes-
sive flashes, were playing on the surface of the
water, which, from a column of perpetually rising
bubbles, appeared to be boiling. The air they contained, ignited as it came in contact with an oven-
like furnace, which the flames fed, and rendered, on
one side red-hot. The heat of this self-ignited
furnace rendered the surface of the water tepid, but
it is naturally cold.   In order to condense, and
thereby perpetuate, the flames, about one-half of
the spring is built over, with an aperture in the
centre of the arch, through which, looking from the
terrace above, the flames are seen playing on the
water. Persons bathing, took in their hands and
on their clothes the water with the flame burning
on it. The uncovered part is a square of less than
five feet, and the covered part about the same di-

mensions. The water is brackish, sulphureous, and chalybeate. A servant drank as much of it as he could hold in both hands united, twice filled, and was so severely purged, that he remained behind, and laid down until its effects went off .... The water of the Balwa koond has an exhilarating effect, occasions a slight headache, and a sensation of fulness, which soon go off. Its effects are diuretic, slightly aperient, and creative of hunger.''[*]

The well outside the Kunda, formed by water issuing from the spring, is called *Básikunda*. Here the devotee first bathes and purifies himself. He then bathes in the Bárabakunda itself inside, and offers *bel* leaves and flowers to the flames to appease the burning god. It is said that at each offer of the *bel* leaves and flowers, the god roars louder to express his satisfaction. Close by are *Dadhíbhairava;* the temple of *Jvalakáli;* and the spring of *Kumári.*

At a nearly similar distance and similarly situated is *Lavanákhya*, the Nuolukka of Captain Pogson and the Naldala Khya of Statistical Report of 1868-9, which differs from Barabakunda in the weakness of its flame and in the increased saltness of its water. The salt-water is used for cooking purposes, though it is said that the salt cannot be eliminated from the water. A tradition prevails that this was tested

[*] Captain Pogson's Narrative during a Tour to Chatoegaon, p. 203.

by Mr. Harvey* when he was Collector of Chittagong, and that he accordingly discharged some
persons arrested for illicit manufacture of salt.
The water, it is said, cures goitre. Around Lavanákhya are the following: *Dadhikunda*, a small well
fed by the stream issuing from Lavanákhya; *Guru-
dhvani*, another Jyotirmaya; *Brahma Kunda*, a hot
spring on the top of a small hill, east of Lavanákhya; *Suryakunda*, a phenomenon similar to Lavanákhya and Bárabakunda.† Near Lavanákhya a
place is shown as where the right arm of Sati, the
consort of Siva, fell, cut by the discus of Vishnu.
But no idol is seen there, and it is not held in the
same veneration as Kálighat, Kámákhyá, and similar
places.

Dr. Oldham thus epitomizes Captain Pogson:
"There are seven other springs within a circle of

* Mr. John Inglis Harvey was Collector of Chittagong from
1831 to 1837, with short intermissions, during which he acted as
Commissioner of the Division. *Vide* Mr. Cotton's Memorandum
on the Revenue History of Chittagong, pp. 118-121.

† There are Mohuntas at the temple of Śambhunath, Bárabakunda, and Lavanákhya. Of those, the Mohunta of Sambhunath
is the richest and the most well-known. He is generally called the
Mohunta of Sitakund. The present Mohunta of Sitakund, whose
name is Kis, or Ban, is a young gentleman of excellent manners,
and of good education. He is also the Mohunta of Ádinath, in
the island of Moisoal. Of this god the same story is told as of
that at Vaidyanath, near Deoghur. The Mohuntas have to take a
vow of celibacy, and are succeeded by their principal disciples.

six miles, called Nuolukka (Lavanákhya), Kooaree (Kumári Kund), Dadhee (Dadhi), Burma (Brahma), Suruj (Súrya), Chandur (Chandra), and Seeta (Síta). Nuolukka is warm, vapour ignites on the application of flame, saline; Kooaree is hot, saline, sulphureous, and chalybeate; vapour ignites. Dadhee, water is cold, salt. Burma (Brahma?) very hot and saltish, slightly chalybeate, vapour ignites. Chandur or Chander is on a hill, salt and exceedingly hot ('said to have appeared within the last four months') ignites; Seeta is pure and limpid.*"

From Lavanákhya the pilgrim proceeds to *Sahasra-dhárá*, a cataract. The water falls beautifully in thin streams, so as to form a natural shower-bath, from a height of about 400 feet. This is by far the most picturesque and romantic of all the various and wonderful sights of Sitakund. It is customary for pilgrims to stand under it. The water of Sahasra-dhárá is considered to be Siva himself. One cannot forget the bath at Sahasradhárá. It is said, that on the words "bom bom," which are peculiar to Siva, being pronounced, the water falls with gradually increasing force.

The places noted before are those generally visited by pilgrims. There are many others, for the *locale* of which the curious and the religious will refer to the *Váráhí Tantra*, the Bradshaw of the shrines of

* Memoirs of the Geological Survey of India, Vol. XIX, Part II, p. 50.

Sitakund.   From what has been said above, the
reader who has - had patience to follow us to the
end of this book, will, it is trusted, be convinced of
the recent character of these shrines.   There is a
sustained effort to plant on this place all the *tirthas*
which are held in esteem by the Hindoos.   For the
most famous shrines of Benares, of Gaya, of Brinda-
van, of Puri, and other places, miniature *tirthas* are
pointed out in Sitakund.*   The remarkable phenomena which nature presents in the place, have aided
the fabrication of superstitious interpolations and
forgeries.   The sacred writings, which have been
quoted before, bear evident indications of the alter-
nate supremacy of the Sivaites and the Vishnuvites, and of the gradual multiplication of the shrines
esteemed by each sect.   But the belief in their
sacredness is firm, deep-rooted, and universal.   A
man who holds a different opinion, is looked upon
as irreligious and sacrilegious, even in Chittagong,
where Hindooism is at a discount.   Whether on
account of their recent establishment, or from any
other cause, the shrines have not received atten-
tion at the hands of the antiquarian and the scien-

* There seems to be no end of places called Sitakund.   In p. 28
ante and footnote, it has already been stated that there are three
more Sitakunds, besides the Sitakund in Chittagong, viz., those at
Monghyr, Kalat, and Ceylon.   In pages 22 and 35 of Vol. XVI of
Cunningham's Archæological Report, there is mention of another
Sitakund situate on the River Gandak in Tirhut.

tist. In these pages they have been described by
a layman. But the antiquarian and the scientist
will be able to ascertain the time when these shrines
were first established, and how they gradually ex-
panded. They will be able to ascertain the effect
of the waters of the several springs, and analyze
the medicinal virtues, which they are believed to
possess. They will be able to ascertain the extent
of the Hindoo occupation of the district, and of its
conquest by the king of Tipperah. They will, in
short, be able to complete the ancient history of
Chittagong, which is now so meagre and unsatis-
factory.